DUNCAN
A Brave Rescue

by Liam O'Donnell   Illustrated by Robert Hynes

AMERICAN VETERINARY MEDICAL ASSOCIATION ®

For Layne, a hero in everybody's eyes — L.O.

To Ellen Gelman — B.H.

Book Copyright © 2004 Trudy Corporation

Published by Soundprints Division of Trudy Corporation, Norwalk, Connecticut.

Book design: Marcin D. Pilchowski
Editor: Laura Gates Galvin
Editorial assistance: Brian E. Giblin

First Edition 2004
10 9 8 7 6 5 4 3 2 1
Printed in China

Acknowledgements:
    Soundprints would like to thank Joanne Clevenger and all the helpful staff and veterinarians at the American Veterinary Medical Association.

Library of Congress Cataloging-in-Publication Data

O'Donnell, Liam, 1970-
        Duncan, a brave rescue / by Liam O'Donnell ; illustrated by Robert Hynes.-- 1st ed.
            p. cm. -- (Pet tales)
        Summary: Duncan, a dalmatian dog who lives in a fire station, has an unexpected opportunity to save puppies from the basement of a burning apartment building.
        ISBN 1-59249-291-6 (large pbk.) -- ISBN 1-59249-292-4 (small pbk.)
        [1. Animal rescue--Fiction. 2. Dalmatian dog--Fiction. 3. Dogs--Fiction. 4. Fire fighters--Fiction.] I. Hynes, Robert, ill. II. Title. III. Series.

PZ7.O2397Du 2004
[E]--dc22
                                                                                2004002586

DUNCAN
A Brave Rescue

by Liam O'Donnell   Illustrated by Robert Hynes

Soundprints

4

The sun rises over the busy city as a Dalmatian wakes from his sleep. With a stretch and a yawn, Duncan is out of his bed and ready to start the day. He trots off to wake the rest of his family.

Duncan lives in a big house with a big family. His home is a fire station and the firefighters are his family.

Duncan scampers into the small sleeping rooms to wake the firefighters. He barks until everyone is awake. Finally, the sleepy firefighters roll out of bed.

Duncan follows the firefighters into the kitchen. Firefighter Andy sets a bowl of food and fresh water down on the floor for Duncan, and then begins making breakfast for the rest of the crew.

The firefighters begin to eat their breakfast, but Duncan is ready to play! He loves to play hide-and-seek. Andy rubs Duncan's neck and tells him to go hide. Duncan races away.

Duncan runs to Andy's fire engine. The fire engine is so big it has two steering wheels! There is one in the front and one in the back. Duncan scrambles into the Tillerman's cabin—the steering cabin in the back of the truck. He hides under the seat and waits for Andy to find him.

Duncan waits and waits, but Andy doesn't find him. He soon forgets about the game and falls asleep under the Tillerman's chair. He no longer wants to be found.

Suddenly, the fire alarm sounds! Duncan wakes up and hears the firefighters jumping into action. They climb into the trucks and zoom out of the station. Duncan is not supposed to be on the truck, but with all the commotion, nobody notices him!

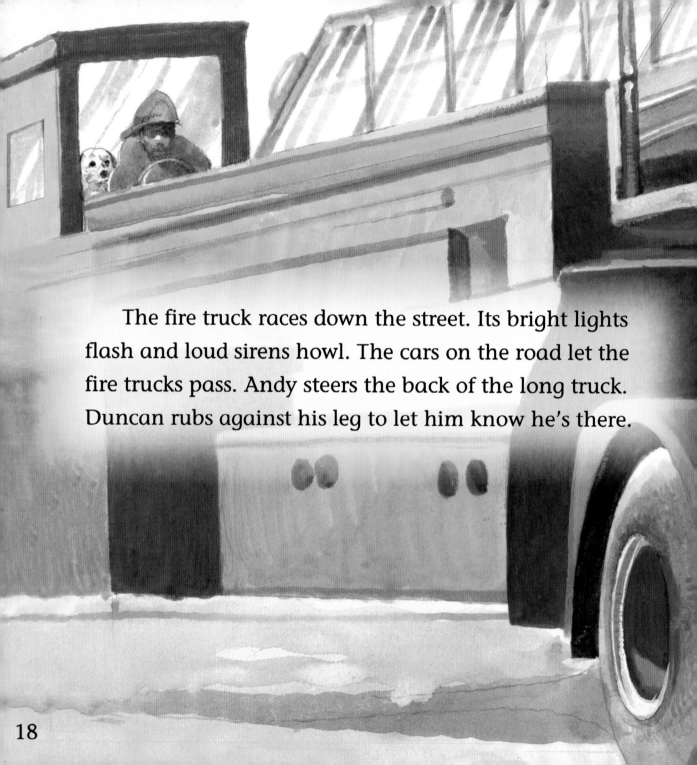

The fire truck races down the street. Its bright lights flash and loud sirens howl. The cars on the road let the fire trucks pass. Andy steers the back of the long truck. Duncan rubs against his leg to let him know he's there.

19

Andy is surprised to see Duncan on the truck. A fire truck is not a safe place for him!

The trucks arrive at a burning apartment building. Andy tells Duncan to stay on the truck where he'll be safe. Through all the noise, Duncan hears barking coming from the building. There are dogs trapped inside!

21

Even though Andy told Duncan to stay on the truck, Duncan jumps down from it and follows the sound of barking coming from a small basement window. Three puppies are trapped inside. Duncan pushes the window open with his nose.

The puppies are too small to reach the window. One by one, Duncan gently lifts the puppies out of the window and sets them down on the grass. After all the puppies are out of the basement, Duncan moves them away from the burning building.

Suddenly, a dog leaps out from a door. It is the puppies' mother, and she is looking for them. The puppies bark loudly and soon their mother sees them. They are all are safe, thanks to Duncan!

Even though Andy is proud of Duncan for his brave rescue, he will be sure that Duncan never gets on the fire truck again.

Back at the firehouse, Andy congratulates Duncan. Duncan is tired from all the excitement of the day. From now on, he'll let the firefighters be the heroes!

Pet Health and Safety Tips

• Your veterinarian can help you develop an evacuation plan for your pets in case of an emergency such as a fire or flood. In addition to several days' worth of food and supplies, your evacuation kit should include a copy of your pet's medical history, including his or her vaccination records. For more help in disaster planning, visit www.avma.org/disaster.

• Identifying your pets will help reunite you with them in the event that you are separated during a disaster. Each pet should have a tag on its collar and a microchip (an electronic identification device) embedded underneath its skin. Visit your veterinarian to have your pet microchipped.

• To maintain the special relationship you have with your pets, you need to provide for their well-being. This means giving them quality food and water, appropriate shelter, proper training and regular veterinary care.

Glossary

Scamper: To move playfully or quickly.

Rescue: To save from danger.

Hero: A person who shows great courage.

Commotion: Noisy confusion.

A REAL-LIFE PET TALE

Sparkler is a real fire-fighting hero in Vancouver, Washington. The four-year-old Dalmatian works with Deputy Fire Marshal Virginia Chapman of the Vancouver fire department teaching fire safety to children. Sparkler shows the boys and girls how to stop, drop and roll and crawl low under smoke. At the fire station, she loves to sit on the fire engines and pose for pictures with visiting children. When she isn't working, Sparkler enjoys playing with her best friend, a white cat!